D0576496

MOUSE

by Todd Starr Palmer
pictures by Judy Lanfredi

Dial Books for Young Readers · New York

To my girls
Gordie, Elsie, Mellie, and Leslee;
and Jake the Snake—T.S.P.

For Dean, with love—J.L.

Published by Dial Books for Young Readers
A Division of Penguin Books USA Inc.
375 Hudson Street
New York, New York 10014

Text copyright © 1994 by Todd Starr Palmer
Pictures copyright © 1994 by Judith M. Lanfredi
All rights reserved / Printed in Hong Kong

The Dial Easy-to-Read logo is a registered trademark of
Dial Books for Young Readers,
A Division of Penguin Books USA Inc., ® TM 1,162,718.

First Edition
1 3 5 7 9 10 8 6 4 2

Library of Congress Cataloging in Publication Data
Palmer, Todd Starr, 1961–   Rhino and Mouse /
Todd Starr Palmer ; pictures by Judy Lanfredi.
p.   cm.
Summary: Rhino's impetuosity and housemate Mouse's
meticulousness clash in comic fashion as the
friends celebrate a holiday, get Rhino out of a tight
spot, and dress up as each other for a costume party.
ISBN 0-8037-1322-3—ISBN 0-8037-1323-1 (lib. bdg.)
[1. Mice—Fiction.   2. Rhinoceroses—Fiction.
3. Friendship—Fiction.]   I. Lanfredi, Judy, ill.
II. Title.   PZ7.P1864Rh 1994 [E]—dc20
93-33299   CIP   AC

The art for each picture was prepared using black pencil,
black ink, and watercolor. It was then color-separated and
reproduced as red, blue, yellow, and black halftones.

Reading Level 2.2

Contents

4

A SPECIAL DAY

Rhino bounced into Mouse's room.

"Rise and shine," sang Rhino.

"Guess what day it is today!"

Mouse opened one sleepy eye.

"What day is today?" asked Mouse.

"It is National Mouse and Rat Day!"

shouted Rhino.

"And guess what else?

I am going to do all the work today."

Mouse tried to go back to sleep.
"I will start by making your bed,"
said Rhino.

Mouse said nothing.

Soon Mouse heard a crash.

"Mouse! Come quickly!" called Rhino.

Mouse ran to the kitchen.

"Your National Mouse and Rat Day

breakfast is ready," said Rhino.

"I made it myself."

"What is it?" asked Mouse.

"It is a fried egg covered with

special sauce," said Rhino.

Mouse took a tiny bite.

"What is the sauce?" he asked.

"Hot fudge and catsup," said Rhino.

Mouse felt a little sick.

Later Mouse walked
into the living room.
Rhino was moving the sofa.
"Where are all my books?"
asked Mouse.
"I am letting them dry," said Rhino.
"Letting them dry?" gasped Mouse.

"Of course," said Rhino.

"You must always dry things after you wash them.

Your books were very dusty."

Mouse's head started to hurt.

In the afternoon Rhino looked

all over the house for Mouse.

"Mouse! Oh, Mouse!" called Rhino.

"Come and see what I did."

He found Mouse and led him outside.

"Surprise!" said Rhino.
"I hope you like dots as
much as I do."

Mouse let out a little moan.

After dinner Rhino handed Mouse a box.

"I bought you a pet today," said Rhino.

"A pet!" said Mouse.

"I have always wanted a pet.

Is it a goldfish or a parrot or..."

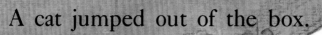
A cat jumped out of the box.

14

Mouse did not move a whisker.

15

Rhino returned the cat to the pet store.

Mouse was in bed when Rhino came home.

"I hope you enjoyed your day,"

said Rhino happily.

"It is too bad that National Mouse and

Rat Day only comes once a year."

Thank goodness, thought Mouse

as he tried to fall asleep.

HORNING IN

One day Mouse was making cheese
toast when he heard someone cry,
"Mouse, Mouse, come help me!"
That sounds like Rhino, thought Mouse.
He always seems to get into trouble
just when we are ready to eat.
Mouse looked all over the house,
but he could not find Rhino.
Finally he looked in the basement.

There was Rhino, standing on his toes.

"What is wrong?" asked Mouse.

"I got my horn stuck in this
silly old pipe," sniffled Rhino.

"Why did you stick your horn
in a pipe?" asked Mouse.

"To see if it would fit!" cried Rhino.

"Does it?" asked Mouse.

"Too well!" wailed Rhino.

"Now will you help me?"

"Of course," said Mouse.

"That is what friends are for."

Mouse sat down to think.

Rhino's horn was stuck in a pipe that
led up to a big jumble of pipes
way above his head.

"Mmmmmmmm," said Mouse.

"I guess we could cut it off."

"CUT IT OFF!" screamed Rhino.

"Please do not cut off my horn!"

"Calm down," said Mouse.

"I meant cut the pipe.

But maybe there is a better way."

"What are you going to do?"
asked Rhino.

Mouse picked up a bottle of
laundry soap.

He squirted it at Rhino until

his snout bubbled with suds.

"Hey! Wait a minute," hollered Rhino.

"This stuff makes my nose itch!"

Rhino sneezed a giant sneeze.

"KAAAACHOO!!"

It knocked Mouse to the floor.

"Oh, I am so mad at you, Mouse,"
sputtered Rhino.

"That soap got up my nose and I...I..."
Suddenly Rhino noticed he was looking
Mouse right in the eye.

"I am *un*-stuck!" said Rhino.

"You made me sneeze myself free!"

Mouse smiled—just a little.

"Thank you!" said Rhino.

"I am so glad we are friends.

You always help me.

And I will always help you."

"Then please stop hugging me,"

gasped Mouse. "I cannot breathe."

"Certainly," said Rhino.

"After all, that is what friends are for."

THE COSTUME PARTY

Rhino ran into the house

waving a letter.

"Look, Mouse," said Rhino.

"Walrus has invited us to her

Cuckoo Costume Party tonight!"

"I love costume parties," said Mouse.

"I wonder who I will be."

"I will be a pirate," shouted Rhino,

"or a sofa or a robot or a..."

"I know what we can do," said Mouse.

"You can be me, and I will be you."

"That will be extra cuckoo for sure!"
said Rhino.

Rhino and Mouse went to work on
their costumes.

Rhino made cardboard ears and whiskers
and found a piece of rope for a tail.
Rhino took seven minutes.
Mouse measured and cut and pinned and
sewed, and made a horn out of clay.
Mouse took four hours.

"Now I look just like you," said Rhino.

"Squeak! Squeak! I am a tiny mouse."

Mouse frowned.

"Mice do not say 'squeak, squeak'

all the time."

"They do too," said Rhino.

"SQUEAK! SQUEAK! SQUEAK!"

"They do not!" said Mouse.

"I am a *real* mouse and I should know.

We only squeak when we get upset."

"Why are you stuffing that pillow
in your costume?" asked Rhino.
"Because you have a big stomach,"
said Mouse.

"I DO NOT!" snorted Rhino.

"I am just big and strong."

"Well, I think you are big and...FAT!"

squeaked Mouse.

Rhino started to cry.

Then Mouse started to cry.

"I am sorry, Rhino.

I did not mean that."

"I am sorry too," said Rhino.

"Sometimes, rhinos who try to be mice

say the wrong things."

"You are my best friend in the whole world," said Mouse.

"Can I still be you?" asked Rhino.

"Of course you can be me," said Mouse.

"You can even squeak—a little.

Can I still be you?"

"You can be me anytime," said Rhino.

That night two best friends went to
the party and had a very good time.